Medieval Tales
That Kids Can Read & Tell

Medieval Tales

That Kids Can Read & Tell

Lorna MacDonald Czarnota

August House Publishers, Inc.

ACKNOWLEDGMENTS
I would like to thank Dr. David Breeden for information about Beowulf, especially the Geat; Tom Heim for sharing his knowledge of Charlemagne and Eleanor of Aquitaine; and Paul Halsall for furthering my knowledge of Saladin.

Published 2000 by August House Publishers, Inc.,
3500 Piedmont Rd., Suite 310, Atlanta, GA 30305
www.augusthouse.com

Printed in the United States of America

LIBRARY OF CONGRESS CATALOGING-IN-PUBLICATION DATA
Czarnota, Lorna.
    Medieval tales for kids to tell / Lorna MacDonald Czarnota.
      p. cm.
    Includes bibliographical references.
    Summary: Presents traditional stories about the Middle Ages along with tips
    for storytellers.
    ISBN 0–87483–589– 2   — ISBN 0–87483–588–7
    1. Middle Ages—Folklore. 2. Tales. [1. Middle Ages—Folklore. 2. Folklore.
    3. Storytelling—Collections.] I. Title.

PZ8.1.C993 Mf2000
398.27—dc21   00-036187

Project Editor: Jody McNeese
Production Editor: Joy Freeman
Cover Artist: Carol Lyon

The paper used in this publication meets the minimum requirements
of the American National Standard for Information Sciences—
Permanence of Paper for Printed Library Materials, ANSI Z39.48-1984.

AUGUST HOUSE   PUBLISHERS   ATLANTA

Dedicated to my parents for the love of reading and learning; the teachers and children who encouraged me to write this book; Tom for being my biggest supporter; Anne, Merri, and Lynn for cheering me on; and Dan Keding, my friend and teacher, for helping me find the courage to do it.

Note to the Student

The stories in this book are just skeletons that give the main ideas. Each storyteller can add his or her own details to make the story unique without losing the point of the story. The tips for telling will help you get started. Each story also includes a history to help you understand the people, culture, and events that may have affected it. Reading the histories as well as the stories will make your stories stronger and more believable. You may want to include some of the history in the stories.

Example: You are telling the story of Robin Hood. You might say something such as, "While our good King Richard is off fighting in the crusades, his brother John is stealing from us. Thank goodness for Robin Hood. Have you heard about Robin?" Then you would tell your story. You gave the audience some history first and helped them believe you really lived in that time and place.

Be sure to read the sections after all the stories, too. You'll find lots of storytelling pointers and ways to become a medieval storyteller. There is also a glossary, which gives the meaning of the *italicized* words in the stories.

And remember: Be creative. Consider different points of view for each story. Have fun with your audience!

Note to the Teacher

Trends in education include total subject immersion for more in-depth learning, a growing interest in language arts and their importance in the curriculum, and cross-curricular activities that make use of a variety of learning skills and information. Social Studies is a good subject for integration of other curricular areas, and storytelling is an excellent device for connecting curricula and meeting Language Arts requirements.

This book makes medieval stories available to students and helps them understand the functions of the medieval storyteller. Students are encouraged to learn the stories and share them with other grade levels as well as their own. Role playing and dressing in costume will add an extra dimension to the experience. You may want to read the "how to" portions of this book with the students, but allow them to make their own story choices.

7

Contents

King Arthur and the Knights of the Round Table: Tales from the Britons

Duke Lech: A Tale from Poland

Beowulf: Tales from the Anglo-Saxons

Charlemagne and the Crusades: A Tale from France

Saladin: A Tale from the Muslims

Alexander the Great: A Tale from Greece

William Tell

A TALE FROM SWITZERLAND

The Legend of William Tell

William was a good man. He lived in Switzerland. One day he took his youngest son into town. As William and his son were walking through the village square, they noticed a hat hanging on a post. The little boy pointed at the hat and William laughed. They continued walking.

Suddenly, a guard shouted, "You there! Come back and bow before the governor's hat!"

William and his son kept walking. Before they knew it, they were surrounded by armed guards. William and his son were arrested. They were taken before the governor.

When questioned, William said what was on his mind. "I will not bow before a hat! I will not give up my freedom!"

"Then," said the governor, "you will shoot an apple from your son's head."

The guards laughed.

"I cannot do that," William protested. "If I miss, I might kill my son."

"Well, if you do not, I will kill your son for you!" the governor threatened.

William's son was brave. He trusted his father. He put an apple on his head and said, "I know you can do it, Father."

William drew two arrows from his quiver and hid one under his cloak. His hands shook as he nocked an arrow and drew the bow. The arrow cut the apple in two. Everyone, except the governor, cheered. The governor was angry and embarrassed. Then he saw the second arrow sticking out of William's cloak.

He laughed at William, saying, "I thought you were such a good shot you would only need one arrow. You must have thought you would need a second try."

William answered slowly, "If I had killed my son, the second arrow

15

would have been for you." He took his son by the hand and led him home.

Aside: And I have heard that he kept that arrow and used it on another day.

Tips for Telling

For very young children, you may want to show them a map and point out Switzerland. Listeners should be impressed with William's son's courage and William's cleverness, so emphasize these parts of the story.

To create suspense, make sure you pause after, "He took his son by the hand and led him home." Look at one member of the audience and say the aside: "And I have heard that he kept that arrow and used it on another day."

Story History

When we study the Middle Ages, we usually think about England, and sometimes France, Italy, and Spain. But there were many other civilizations in existence around the world. There were Native Americans in the New World even before the Europeans discovered America. There were many people living in Africa and China, as well as other places. There were many smaller countries experiencing the Middle Ages, such as Germany and Poland. There was also Switzerland, the place of William Tell's birth.

Peasants like William were considered the property of the lords who ruled the land. The governor in this story was the ruler of William's home. He made the laws and people obeyed them or were severely punished. William was a *freeborn peasant*. He was not a *serf*. Serfs were like slaves. They had no rights. But even William could be punished by the governor. Fortunately, the governor was too afraid of William.

Robert Bruce

A TALE FROM SCOTLAND

Robert and the Spider

Robert, king of Scotland, was fighting a hard war against the English. He was losing.

Six times his armies had gone to battle, and six times they had lost. Now they were scattered and it seemed hopeless. Robert Bruce was forced to hide in the woods. He found an old tumble-down shed. He put his blanket on the floor and fell onto it, exhausted. He was tired and hungry. He felt discouraged.

Many days passed. One day, as he sat listening to the rain fall outside the shed, he noticed a little spider making her web in the corner of the ceiling.

The little spider patiently made one strand and then another. Finally she tried to catch hold of a ceiling beam over Robert's head. The web broke, and she hung in midair. Again she tried, and again she failed. Six times that little spider shot out her silken strand. Six times she failed.

"Poor thing," Robert said. "You will fail, as I have failed."

But the little spider kept trying. On the seventh try, her thread held fast, and the little spider climbed easily overhead.

All at once Robert jumped to his feet. "I too will try a seventh time. Thank you, little friend!"

The spider gave Robert new hope. He rounded up his men and sent messengers all across the countryside. Soon a large army of brave Scotsmen gathered around him. Robert fought a seventh battle against the English. Afterward, the English were very happy to return to their own country and leave the Scots alone. Scotland was free.

Aside: And I have heard it said that Robert never harmed, nor would he allow others to harm, a spider after that.

19

Tips for Telling

If you are telling to children in grade four and up, you might ask them if they saw the movie *Braveheart*. They might recognize Robert Bruce and William Wallace from the movie. The movie writers did a good job researching their history, but they changed a few facts to make the movie more interesting. The costumes and events were very good examples of historical fact mixed with fiction.

Story History

Robert Bruce (sometimes called Robert the Bruce) was a Scottish nobleman who was destined to become king of Scotland. There were several men in Robert's family named Robert Bruce, because sons were named for their fathers. The Robert in this story was known as Robert I.

The English ruled over Scotland for many years. After the death of William Wallace, a Scottish outlaw who began an uprising against the English, Robert Bruce was finally crowned king of Scotland. Now he faced the difficult task of finishing what Wallace started. But the English were strong and came in great numbers. Scotland did finally win its independence. Years later, it became part of what is now called Great Britain. It is under English law once again.

Robin Hood

TALES FROM ENGLAND

Robin Meets a Giant

There was no place for Robin Hood to live now that Prince John had taken his father's home. So Robin lived in the forest of Sherwood. It was a dark and dense forest and hard for John's men to search completely. It was easy for Robin to hide and make mischief for John and his men.

The story of Robin of Locksley was soon heard by the peasants who were bullied by the Sheriff of Nottingham. They were being treated poorly and overtaxed. It did not take long for them to join Robin in his fight against the sheriff's tyranny. They came in small groups or one at a time. Soon Robin had many followers. They became known as Robin's Merry Men.

One day, as Robin walked alone in the forest, he came to a stream. A tree had fallen over it. Robin decided to use it as a bridge. He was only halfway across when a huge man carrying a *quarterstaff* jumped from the bushes. That man was at least one foot taller than Robin. His arms were thick, and his thighs were as big around as Robin's waist. He had a grizzled beard and one tooth missing.

"Hold there!" the large man cried.

"Out of my way, oaf," Robin answered, but the large man stood his ground. "Very well, I will have to teach you a lesson." Robin found a tree branch and used it as a weapon.

"Maybe it will be you who will learn the lesson!" the larger man shouted and thrust forward with his staff.

The blow sent Robin wheeling, but he regained his footing and fought back with all his might.

The two men tousled. First one thrust his weapon, then the other. Finally, the giant hit Robin so hard that he fell from the bridge into the icy water.

The giant reached to help his fallen opponent. Robin gripped his hand tightly, and with one last solid yank, the larger man was pulled in beside him. They fought with their hands. Then the giant began to laugh. He laughed so hard he could not stop. His belly shook. His laughter rumbled.

Soon Robin was laughing too. "Well met, good man. Tell me, what is thy name?"

"John Little," said the giant.

"John Little? More like Little John," laughed Robin.

"And how about you?"

Robin held out his hand in friendship and grasped Little John's elbow. "Robin Hood."

"Bless me," said Little John. "You are just the man I was coming to find." Little John fell to his knees. "Take me as one of your men, and I promise to serve you until I die. Which, I hope, is not too soon."

Robin took Little John as his first man and seldom were the two seen apart after that day.

Tips for Telling

When Robin meets Little John, exaggerate the large man's size. Make him sound amazing. Also, make the fight between the men playful. Robin was known for liking a good fight, a good joke, and a brave man.

Robin Goes Fishing

It was a bright, sunny, warm spring day. Robin and his men were on their way to cause more trouble for the Sheriff of Nottingham when they heard the sound of snoring coming from behind a large tree. Robin gave his men a signal to be quiet and went to investigate. There, leaning against the tree, his hood pulled down over his eyes, was a round little friar. He held a fishing line in one chubby hand and a greasy leg of *mutton* in the other.

Without making a sound, Robin reached out and took the fishing line. He whispered to his men, "Looks like we caught a fat fish."

But the friar did not wake. Then Robin grabbed the leg of mutton. As soon as he touched it, the friar woke.

Robin drew his sword.

"Would you harm a helpless friar?" asked the round little man.

"Friar?" exclaimed Robin. "I think you are more a mule, my friend. On your feet and carry me across the stream."

The friar could not protest because he was outnumbered. He got to his feet, and Robin climbed on his back.

"Now off with you!" shouted Robin, digging his heels into the friar's sides like a horse.

The friar carried Robin out into the middle of the stream, grunting and bending under Robin's weight. Then, all of a sudden, he straightened his back with force, and Robin went flying into the water. SPLASH! In an instant, the friar took a sword from under his cloak and forced Robin to the opposite side of the stream. Sputtering and spitting water, Robin climbed to the shore.

"Now who is the mule?" growled the friar.

Robin was forced to carry the friar back to the outlaw camp, where Friar

Tuck finally introduced himself. Robin apologized for being rude, and the two men became fast friends.

From that day on, although Robin continued to tease the friar, he respected him. And Friar Tuck shared many great adventures with Robin Hood, Lord of Sherwood.

Tips for Telling

Friar Tuck is always shown as a round little man with a love of food and drink. He is also shown to be rather persistent. He could joke with Robin, but he was also a tough fighter.

Story History

Robin Hood probably never really lived. Storytellers and *balladeers* most likely made up the stories of Robin Hood by combining several folk heroes into one. However, Nottingham and Sherwood Forest are real places. And King Richard and his brother, Prince John, were also real.

One of the tricks that good writers and storytellers can use is including fact with fiction. Whenever real places, people, and events are mixed with fiction, people who are listening to or reading the stories are more likely to believe they are real.

Richard Lion-Heart, whom Robin loved, was the son of Eleanor of Aquitaine and King Henry II. None of their children were perfectly good people. Even Richard, who is shown to be a good king, was influenced by the prejudices of his culture. During the Middle Ages, there was much prejudice against women, the poor, and those of faiths other than Christian. Perhaps it was because life was so difficult that legends such as those of Robin Hood became popular. The common people needed a hero.

A common custom in medieval warfare was to capture noblemen and hold them for ransom. In fact, any other treatment would have been considered less than honorable for noblemen and knights.

King Richard was off fighting in the crusades with the rest of his knights. He was on the way home when he was taken prisoner by the Duke of Austria. He seemed to vanish. The people of England thought their king was dead. His brother John hoped he was because then John could put the crown on his own head. The saying goes, "When the cat's away, the mice will play." John was having a wonderful time gaining power and wealth while the Lion-Heart was gone.

The people were miserable. Especially those who lived under the law of Nottingham and its sheriff. They were overtaxed and cruelly treated. The people were starving.

Word finally arrived at the castle that Richard was not dead. He was being held for an enormous ransom by the Austrians. When Richard's people heard this, they demanded action. Their king must be rescued at all costs. And so the task was set: a ransom had to be collected, and the best method at that time for raising money was taxation. But much of the money never made it into the king's treasury. Instead, it found its way into the pockets of Prince John and his loyal followers.

Because of this, the demand for taxes continued to grow. But there was little hope they would ever raise enough to save Richard. A hero was needed. That hero was Robin Hood.

Robin of Locksley, or Robin Hood, was a loyal subject of the king. His father was also loyal, but he was murdered by traitors. His father's lands and properties were taken from Robin by Prince John in an effort to remove power from his brother's supporters. Robin decided to fight Prince John. He became an outlaw and was known as Robin of the Hood for the hooded clothing he wore. This was later shortened to Robin Hood.

Many kinds of men came into the service of Robin Hood: poor peasants and serfs, fighting men like Little John, minstrels such as Will Scarlet, and a fat old friar named Friar Tuck. He didn't know he would come into Robin's service, but he did. Tuck was one of England's finest swordsmen. That may surprise you, but many friars found it necessary to defend themselves. Even though men of religion were peaceful, the medieval world was not. There were robbers on the roads that did not steal from the rich and give to the poor like Robin. There were also invaders who attacked, robbed, and destroyed the churches and monasteries. Many monks and friars like Tuck were killed, especially those who did not know how to defend themselves.

Joan of Arc

TALES FROM FRANCE

Joan the Maid Meets the Dauphin

Joan was thirteen years old when she first heard the voices. She said the voices were messengers from God. They told her that she would save France. At first, she did not want to listen. But finally Joan cut her hair and dressed like a boy. In this way she could move about the country safely. She traveled to the *Dauphin's** palace.

The Dauphin heard she was coming. He decided to play a trick on her. "We will see if this girl has God on her side," he told the people in his court. "She is probably just a beggar. I will offer her money and she will go away." Everyone laughed.

The Dauphin changed clothes with a friend. His friend, dressed like the prince, sat on the throne while the true Dauphin hid in the crowd. But Joan was not to be fooled.

She walked past the throne and up to the real Dauphin, fell to her knees, and said, "I am Joan the Maid, and I have come to save France."

Everyone was amazed that she could pick the Dauphin out of the crowd at the palace.

The Dauphin did not want to believe her. Then Joan whispered a secret in his ear. Only he could have known that secret, which has never been discovered. The Dauphin was forced to believe her. Once the Dauphin's clergymen questioned Joan about her voices, she was given a horse, a banner, armor, and a beautiful sword—the sword of Saint Catherine. It had five crosses on the blade and had been hidden in a church under the altar. Now the Dauphin let Joan lead his armies. The Maid, a peasant girl just thirteen years old, was in charge of France's army!

* Dauphin is pronounced *DAW-fin.*

31

Tips for Telling

Remember point-of-view when telling this story. Joan was a hero to the French people. She was an enemy to the English. This is when it helps to know which side you are on when telling the story. You may also want to tell the audience that "dauphin" means "prince."

The Battle of Orleans

The Battle of Orleans* was an important battle. If the French could keep this city from the English, they might win the whole war. But Joan and her army were losing. The English were pushing them further and further back.

Joan watched as her men began to tire. Many wanted to retreat or surrender. The situation was desperate, but Joan, who was fifteen years old at this time, was not about to give up. She hoped to inspire her army. Joan took off her helmet so her men could see her face. She picked up her banner and charged into the middle of the battle. Men were fighting and dying all around her.

Joan waved her banner and shouted, "Onward! Onward for glory!"

"Hurrah! Hurrah for Joan!" her men cried. *"Vive Jeanne!"**

An English archer in a siege-tower saw Joan. He nocked an arrow and shot her in the shoulder. Joan was brave, and although it hurt, she did not fall or cry. Joan reached up and pulled the arrow out by herself. Her men were so inspired that they charged forward and won the day.

Tips for Telling

If you choose to tell the Battle of Orleans without telling the story of how Joan meets the Dauphin, you should give the audience some background about Joan. Perhaps you can tell them that Joan was a young girl who convinced the Dauphin that she could save France from the English

---

* Orleans is pronounced *or-lay-OWN*.
  Vive Jeanne is pronounced *VEE-vuh JUN*.

invaders, and Joan now led the whole French army. Make a big deal of how unusual it was for women—especially peasant girls—to do this in the Middle Ages.

Story History

The King of France was dead, and his son, the Dauphin, did not want to be king. Being king was difficult work, and the Dauphin was lazy. It was easier and safer to stay at his palace in southern France. There, he spent the money from his people's taxes and played games while the English took more and more of his country. This was during the Hundred Years War. The people did not know what to do.

Throughout history, the English and the French have attacked each other and taken each other's land. If you look at a map, you will see that the English Channel is just a small body of water separating the two countries. It was easy to cross, and since the Dauphin did not care, the English were winning.

In the Middle Ages, women had little power or control over their lives. The class system also made it impossible for a peasant to be anything more than a peasant. If one were born a peasant, one died a peasant. This makes the story of Joan of Arc even more interesting. She was a girl and, indeed, a young one. Not only that, she was a peasant.

Joan was born in the village of Domremy in northeastern France in the year 1412. She was the daughter of a farmer, and when she was nine years old, Joan could spin wool using a drop spindle. This was common work for young girls to do.

Religion was of great importance during the Middle Ages. People relied on their religion for many reasons, including helping them face the hardships of the Middle Ages. Their religion was comforting. Joan was religious like any other young peasant girl of her time. She prayed in her garden every day from the time she was a young child until she left home. She prayed all her life.

It was unusual for women to travel and even more unusual for peasants to hold titles. But Joan's story is unique. After her death, the Dauphin, who had been crowned king because of Joan's success at Orleans, gave Joan's family a noble title. He also freed her village from paying royal taxes.

The story of Joan's death is tragic. We are usually told that Joan was found guilty of witchcraft. People did believe in witches, and many women were tried, found guilty, and burned at the stake. Yet, the Church was not able to prove that Joan was a witch. The Holy Roman Church in England found Joan guilty of *heresy*.* That means disobeying the law of the Church. That is what her enemies had hoped for.

The Church during the Middle Ages held much power and finally trapped Joan with a law that said a woman could not dress like a man. When told that she must put on a dress, Joan refused. This was just an excuse used by the Church. The politicians used the Church for their own needs.

Joan was a threat to the English, and it was the English who wanted her dead. In fact, the English feared Joan so much that, after her death, they threw her ashes in the Seine* River. They were afraid the French people would be inspired by her. They were right. Her death only made the people stronger against the English. Eventually the Church made Joan a saint, and we know her as Saint Joan of Arc.

---

* Heresy is pronounced *HARE-uh-see*.
  Seine is pronounced *SANE*.

King Arthur and the Knights of the Round Table

TALES FROM THE BRITONS

Sir Gawain Gets Married

Of all the knights at Arthur's Round Table, Sir Gawain* was the most noble. He was the bravest and the most honorable.

One day King Arthur told Gawain of a promise he made to a lady in the forest. "I promised you would marry this lady because she saved my life."

Sir Gawain was ready to serve his king. Arthur took him to meet the lady. She was the ugliest woman Gawain had ever seen. The lady had the nose of a wild pig. Her hair was dirty and crawling with bugs. Her skin was covered with sores. And she smelled terrible.

Sir Gawain could have run away, but a promise was a promise, and neither Arthur nor Gawain could take it back.

Gawain took the lady's hand and kissed it. "I will gladly marry you."

If you have ever been to a wedding, you know there is usually great celebration, but this one was quiet and nobody could eat—except the lady. She ate her food with her bare hands. The grease ran down her arms. Drool ran down her chin. Then it was time for the bride and groom to go to their room.

When they were alone, the lady asked, "Are you going to kiss me?"

Gawain wrinkled his nose. What choice did he have? He closed his eyes and kissed her cheek.

"What kind of kiss is that for your new wife?" the lady complained.

Sir Gawain plugged his nose and kissed her lips. Suddenly, the room was filled with the scent of wildflowers. When he opened his eyes and looked, he could not believe what he saw. A beautiful woman sat before him.

"Who are you?" he asked.

* Gawain is pronounced *guh-WANE*.

"I am your wife. You have broken the spell put on me by my brother, the Green Knight."

Gawain was happy. Then she added, "But I can only be beautiful part of the day. You must choose. Would you have me beautiful by day and ugly by night? Or ugly by day and beautiful at night when we are alone?"

What could Gawain say? How could he tell her what to do? "My lady," he said, "this is your choice, not mine."

The lady smiled. "You have made me very happy. For, by giving me what a woman wants most, the right to choose for herself, you have broken the whole spell. Now I will be beautiful always."

And from that time until the end of time, Gawain and his wife lived happily ever after.

Tips for Telling

Have fun making the lady sound disgusting. Your audience will love it. And you might give her a rough voice until she is beautiful.

King Arthur Meets Excalibur

King Arthur, King of all the Britons, handed Merlin the sword he pulled from the stone—the sword that made him king.

Merlin, the wizard of Arthur's court, pointed his finger toward a wall of mist that surrounded a lake beyond the trees. Arthur walked with his hands in front to show they were empty in respect for that ancient place.

He stood with his head bowed in the silent early morning at the water's edge. Slowly, the sun burned away the mist and the crisp air began to warm. Arthur heard the many birds that surrounded the place as they sang their morning songs to the earth.

Suddenly, the hair on Arthur's neck bristled. Something was about to happen. He saw the water move in ripples, but there was nothing there to make it move—no fish, no bird, no boat. Slowly, a sword rose from the water. It was held by the softest, whitest hand Arthur had ever seen.

"Lady," Arthur whispered.

"Take it!" shouted Merlin from behind him. "Quickly!"

Arthur's hands trembled as he waded into the clear lake waters to take the sword. His fingers just touched the fingers of that soft white hand.

As his hand closed about the hilt of the sword, the Lady-of-the-Lake disappeared beneath the surface. Arthur did not see her but he sensed her beauty. That feeling stayed with him for many days that followed.

When Arthur returned to shore, Merlin was waiting. "This is the sword Excalibur, meant only for you, Arthur."

The king held the sword blade up. "This sword will gain me many victories over my enemies," he said.

"This sword has the power to heal your enemies," said Merlin. The wizard shook his head. "You still have much to learn, my king."

The sword shone with an inner light. It came to life in Arthur's hand.

"Excalibur," Arthur whispered. "Excalibur."

Excalibur was with Arthur until the moment of his death when it was returned to the Lady-of-the-Lake forever. It is said that Arthur will return again someday, and she keeps the sword for him.

Tips for Telling

The more detail and description you give in this story about the place, the Lady, and the feelings of the moment, the more magical the story will be. The lake, the Lady, and the sword are loaded with magic and intense beauty.

Story History

Like Robin Hood, King Arthur probably was not a real man. There was a King Arthur, but he was not like the one in the stories. Storytellers probably made stories of Arthur and his knights out of many different people. These stories date to times before Christianity, and there are hundreds of variations.

Some people have been looking for *Camelot** and the mystical island of *Avalon** for years. Some people think that the hill on which the church of Glastonbury sits is Avalon and the burial place of Arthur and Guenevere.* They actually found the bodies of a king and queen in a tomb in that place. Did these places really exist? They have never been found.

Many characters in the Arthurian legends have mythological beginnings. The Green Knight may be one of the many *Celtic** gods of the forest. Dame Ragnell, the Green Knight's sister who marries Sir Gawain, may be a Celtic goddess of spring. The Lady-of-the-Lake was more than likely a water spirit or goddess. And the magical sword Excalibur may be one of the four gifts given to the Celts by the Tuatha de Danann.*

The Tuatha De Danann were ancient gods, later called the fairies, who

---

* Camelot is pronounced *CAM-uh-lot.*
Avalon is pronounced *AV-uh-lawn.*
Guenevere is pronounced *GWIN-uh-VEER.*
Celtic is pronounced *KELT-ic* and Celts is pronounced *KELTS.*
Tuatha de Danann is pronounced *TOO-uh-thuh duh DAW-non.*

lived under the ground in great hills called Sidhe* mounds. Sidhe is another word for "fairy."

When King Arthur was born, Ireland, Scotland, Wales, and England did not exist as individual countries. The people of these places came to be called the Celts, but we should keep in mind that they are different cultures with some similarities. The Celtic people have a long history that includes being a people of many clans and tribes, much like the American Indians. They fought amongst themselves and had no central king. They were hopeful that someone like Arthur could unite them, which may be one of the reasons the Arthurian stories became popular. The Celts were once called the Britons, which should not be confused with Britain, although the root word is the same.

Arthur was a young man when he accidentally discovered his true birthright as King of the Britons. This happened in a story where Arthur pulled a sword from a stone to replace one he had lost. The sword was stuck in the stone magically by Merlin. Whoever removed it would be king. It was the first of two swords used by Arthur.

Another character who is written about in these legends is Merlin, the wizard. Merlin actually means "wizard" in the Gaelic* language of the early Celts. So, there are confusing stories about Merlin, who may actually be many different wizards. The Merlin of these stories was a *druid** and Arthur's advisor.

---

* Sidhe is pronounced *SHEE.*
  Gaelic is pronounced *GAY-lick.*
  Druid is pronounced *DREW-id.*

Duke Lech

A TALE FROM POLAND

A TALE FROM POLAND

Lech and the Nest

Duke Lech* was a hunter, and he loved his hunting birds. But there was one bird that he did not have—he wanted to capture an eagle.

One fine morning the duke went hunting with the men of his court. It was a good hunting day, but Lech was bored. All of a sudden he got an idea. Lech dug his heels into his horse's side and rode off. He left the other men behind. They followed to make sure their duke was safe but let him have plenty of space. He had a bad temper at times.

Lech rode as fast as his horse could carry him until he came to a rocky mountain. He stopped and climbed on foot. He wanted to be far away from the others so he could think. Up and up he went. As he neared the top of the mountain, Lech saw an eagle's nest. A milk-white mother eagle sat feeding her young. When she heard Lech, she turned and screeched at him. The mother eagle was angry. Lech knew he was in trouble. He drew his dagger. He would take a young eagle to train for hunting. It would be strong and powerful. But the mother eagle was not going to make the task easy for Lech. She made that very clear. He would have to get past her first.

Lech raised the dagger and lunged forward. The eagle lifted her powerful wings and beat them in Lech's face. She pecked at him with her beak. She threatened him with her razor-sharp talons.

The duke fought back, striking with his dagger. The two were a blur of hair and feather, beak and blade. Finally, Lech thrust upward and struck the mother eagle in the breast. Her white feathers turned bright red. There was blood on Lech's blade. Still, the wounded eagle pecked at Lech. She was brave and proud. She continued to protect her young.

The eaglets were within Lech's grasp. One last blow and the mother

* Lech is pronounced *LEK*.

47

would not be in his way. But Lech did not kill her. He stepped down from the stone perch. He bowed slightly to the brave eagle. He was ashamed of what he had done.

The duke walked back down the mountain. He left the eagles in peace. The mother would heal. Lech would not take an eaglet.

His *courtiers** finally caught up with their leader. They were waiting when he came down the mountain. They saw a strange look in his eyes. Something had happened.

Lech explained. "There is a brave eagle on this mountain and she has taught me something of importance. She has reminded me of our people. They are brave and they will protect these lands even to the death. Let us build a great city here and let us call it Gniezno*—the Eagle's Nest. And," he said, "let us raise a new banner over her walls—a blood red *field* with a white eagle."

That is how the city of Gniezno and Poland's national emblem came to be!

Tips for Telling

Poland is one of those countries we seldom think of as part of the Middle Ages, and many young children may never have heard of Poland. It may help to show them a map of Europe so they can see where Poland is.

Like most of the stories in this book, different versions of this story exist. I have combined the ones that I liked the best. You may want to find other versions and retell it in your own way. You also might want to find a picture of Lech's eagle flag to show the younger children. Poland has a new flag, but the white eagle is still the national emblem.

Story History

Poland has a rich history before, during, and after the Middle Ages. There are many medieval castles, monasteries, and cities in Poland.

Warsaw and Krakow* are two of its largest cities with castles. Warsaw is actually two cities—Old Town and New Town. Much of New Town was

* Courtiers is pronounced *COURT-ee-urs*.
  Gniezno is pronounced *gun-YEZ-no*.
  Krakow is pronounced *CRACK-ow*.

built by the Russians following World War II. Old Town is a rebuilt medieval city. It was completely destroyed during World War II, but sketches and enough detail in old writings were found to rebuild it using the rubble and some new materials. The streets in Old Town are narrow and paved in stone. There is a central market square with an old medieval fountain used by people and animals. It's very beautiful and includes the home of a very famous woman—Madame Marie Curie, who was Polish and married to a Frenchman. They are known for their work with radioactivity. Marie was born after the Middle Ages in a medieval house.

Krakow, the other major city, has a grand castle that is the burial place of Poland's kings and queens. The castle even has a treasure room. Some stories tell of a dragon that lived beneath this castle!

Krakow also has a marketplace with a large *guild* hall that was used for making and dealing in fine cloth during the Middle Ages. And there is a legend surrounding Krakow's great cathedral. When Poland was attacked by a band of *Tartars** in the thirteenth century, the bugler in the church tower sounded an alarm. He was shot through the neck by an arrow in the middle of his song. Every day—even to this day—a bugler climbs the tower, begins to play, and stops in the exact place where that bugler was killed all those centuries ago. The Polish people are people of long-lasting traditions.

Poland's people have always been known for their strength of character, bravery, and artistic abilities. They fought off the Tartars and other warring peoples, not to mention surviving the horrors of World War II.

According to the legends of the founding of Gniezno, which is another of Poland's medieval cities, Duke Lech had two brothers, Czech and Rus, who went on to found Czechoslovakia* and Russia. Like most legends, we can find truths in these stories.

The eagle flag was used for centuries but was changed in the early 1990s. Today's Polish flag is white on top and red on the bottom. The eagle remains Poland's national emblem, and many Poles still use the eagle flag.

* Tartars is pronounced *TAR-ters*.
Czechoslovakia is pronounced CHECK-*uh-sluh-*VAW-*key-uh*.

Beowulf

TALES FROM THE ANGLO-SAXONS

The Slaying of Grendel

The hall of King Hrothgar* was haunted—not by a ghost, but by fear: fear of being devoured by a mighty monster known as Grendel.* He came each night from the *moor*. He slid silently, dragging one leg behind him as he walked. Grendel was ten feet tall. He had great hairy arms and long slimy teeth. His claws were sharp and dangerous. Even the king's best men could not defeat him.

The beast wandered the land every night. He always came to the king's hall seeking food to eat. Each night, the king's men slept in that place. Grendel would smell them and drool would run from his mouth.

Each night, Grendel would slam his fist into the door and cave it in. The monster would quickly scoop up the first man and eat him alive, then another, and another! He would eat them before anyone could cry for help. Sometimes, that horrible beast would drag a man to his lair beneath the dark water of the moor and keep him there for a tasty morsel at a later time.

The king was beside himself with grief. He had lost many good men, but he was helpless to do anything about it. His once happy hall was now silent.

Storytellers, minstrels, and travelers brought news of this foul creature to many lands. Many heroes tried to help the king. None were successful. Finally, the news came to Beowulf of Geat.* He was the mightiest of heroes. He immediately took his men to help the king.

When Beowulf arrived, the king and queen greeted him with food and gifts of gold and silver. Beowulf promised on his sword to slay the beast and free the land. The king and queen were pleased. They gave Beowulf

---

* Hrothgar is pronounced *RAWTH-gar*.
  Grendel is pronounced *GREN-dull*.
  Beowulf of Geat is pronounced *BAY-uh-woolf of GEET*.

everything he needed. That night, Beowulf told his men to sleep in the hall of the king. But he did not sleep. He only pretended to sleep. Beowulf sat quietly waiting and watching in the darkness.

Then, late in the night—BAAM!—down came the door and in stepped Grendel. Beowulf waited patiently. Grendel grabbed the first man and ate him, arms and legs and all. Beowulf's men jumped to their feet, weapons in hand. They waited for their leader's orders. Beowulf leapt in front of Grendel. He decided to use his hands because the beast used only its hands. This was an honorable fight!

In a flash, Grendel had Beowulf in his sharp claws, but Beowulf grabbed Grendel's arm. The two struggled long and hard. Beowulf was stronger than any other man alive and finally broke free. He twisted the creature's arm and tore it off! Grendel screamed so loudly the sound was heard for miles and miles. It was heard in the dark waters of the moor where his mother slept on top of her great treasure.

Beowulf stood holding Grendel's bloody arm. He hung it from the ceiling. The monster ran off to his den, never to be seen again. There he died.

The king and queen were very grateful to Beowulf for his courage. They rewarded him with much treasure and a beautiful jeweled sword. A feast was held in Beowulf's honor that lasted four days.

Grendel's mother saw to it that the celebration did not last any longer. But that is another story.

Tips for Telling

This is a fun, scary, adventurous story. It should be told with excitement and suspense. If you speed up your words, you can create excitement in your voice. Just make sure you speak clearly so the audience can understand you. If you slow down your words, you will create suspense. Try slowing down for the last two lines: "Grendel's mother saw to it that the celebration did not last any longer. But that is another story."

This is not a good story for very young children. I would tell it to grade four and up. Remember, part of a good storyteller's job is to choose the right story for the right audience.

Have fun describing the monster and use some of your own words when you talk about him. Watch out for words that sound too modern. A medieval storyteller would not use the word "gross," for instance. Instead he or she might say "gruesome" or "hideous."

If you mention Grendel's mother and say, "But that is another story," your listeners may want to hear a second story. If you don't know the story of Grendel's mother, leave that part out.

A Mother's Revenge

Beowulf was a hero to everyone but the monster's mother. She was not happy about her son's death. She was determined to get revenge. She was a creature of darkness.

Grendel's mother entered the king's hall. The men ran for their weapons, but the beast was too quick. She grabbed her son's arm from the ceiling and swung it with great force. She killed the king's best warrior and dearest friend. Then, Grendel's mother ran away.

Beowulf, with the king and his men by his side, rode in pursuit of Grendel's mother. They followed her to her lair in the dark mucky waters of the swamp. It was a horrible place. Beowulf's men were afraid. There were strange lights glowing dimly below the surface, and the place was crawling with frightful demons. Slimy, ugly creatures crawled over the rocks. Inhuman screeches filled the air. But Beowulf, the hero, was not afraid. In his armor with his sword, he dove into the murky waters. Beowulf swam past the strange glowing lights and creatures.

It did not take long for him to find Grendel's mother. She waited in the shadows. As he approached, she raked him with her mighty claws and tried to tear his armor. She dragged him to her den. Beowulf could not draw his sword. The beast rolled Beowulf over and over, trying to drown him. He was strong and held his breath. Beowulf struggled free. He drew his sword and lunged for her heart. The sword could not pierce her hardened skin. As they fought, the muddy bottom swirled upward like a cloud. Man and beast, beast and man struggled for victory. The water was on fire with the heat of battle. It was a storm without an end, a night without a day.

Finally, Beowulf wrestled Grendel's mother to the floor and pinned her there. She struggled and began to wriggle free. Just then, the hero saw a magic sword hanging on the wall. It was the sword of ancient giants and too huge for any ordinary human to wield. But then, Beowulf was no ordinary human, was he?

He grabbed the sword and, in one swift movement, drove it into the monster's heart. Blood swirled upward mixing with the clouds of mud. Then a calm settled on the surface. Beowulf's men and King Hrothgar waited, but Beowulf did not appear. They thought their hero was slain. His men bowed their heads in sadness. Never would they have great adventures again.

Was he slain? No! He burst to the surface, taking a deep breath of life-giving air. "Hurrah!" his men cheered.

Now the king's hall was truly rid of the evil that lurked in its corners. Beowulf and his men were handsomely rewarded and sailed homeward. But heroes always go on to other adventures, as you know. And Beowulf was truly a hero.

Tips for Telling

As with Grendel's story, use the speed with which you tell the tale to help build suspense or make some places more exciting. Slow down for the mysterious parts of the story. Speed up for the more adventurous parts.

Asides help you draw the audience into the story and get them involved in cheering for the hero. When describing Grendel's mother you could say, "If you think Grendel was mean and ugly, you should have seen his mother. His mother was ten times taller and meaner than a dragon with indigestion." You don't have to use asides unless you want to. Make your own anywhere you think it will work best for you. Asides help the audience feel like part of the story.

Also, feel free to use your own descriptions of Grendel and his mother. Change my words and create your own battle details. These stories should be fun to tell. Don't feel you have to memorize the way I wrote them. Remember, I wrote these stories in brief form so you can add details and make them your own.

Beowulf Slays Grendel

A POEM

Hrothgar's hall sat silent,
Where once it had been happy.
Grendel from the darkest depths,
Its greatest warriors slew.
Alone. Afraid. The good king wept.
Songs and stories, minstrels sang.
And word fell on a hero's ear.
Beowulf sailed forth.
Arrived at gate of Herot* Hall,
Announced and gifted by the king
And his good wife,
Beowulf, hero of the Geat,
Promised peace for all within.
His men he scattered about the hall.
Himself slept not that night,
But waited in the dark for death.
Within the moor a monster stirred,
Its heart was turned toward evil deeds.
And Grendel growled and gruesome groped,
Sniffed and snorted in the depths,
The creature slunk and slithered forth,
To feed again at Herot Hall.

* Herot is pronounced *hair-UHT.*

Beowulf felt the beast's hot breath,
And watched as with a sharpened claw,
The creature slew and ate a man,
Beowulf leapt up and stood opposed.
Struggled, strangled, stretched,
Beyond the limit of an ordinary man,
The two bested each other in their strength.
Turned and twisted, terribly,
The hero pulled at Grendel's arm,
And took it off!
The beast let out a cry of pain,
That echoed through the hall and moor,
And stirred his mother from her sleep.
Her son was dead.
Beowulf held his trophy up,
And from the rafters of the hall,
The arm was hung.
And making merry with his men,
Was Beowulf victorious.
And peaceful nights would come again,
At last to Herot Hall.
But then…

A Challenge

If you enjoyed reading my version of this epic-style poem, I challenge you to write one of your own for either Grendel's story or that of Grendel's mother. The difference between a poem and a prose story is that you will need to memorize the poem.

Story History

The Norse culture has a wealth of mythology, bronze work, fine jewelry, and some of the world's finest shipbuilding. The Norsemen came from the Scandinavian countries of Norway, Sweden, and Denmark. To be a Norseman means to come from the north (to be a North man). The story of

Beowulf mentions his home, Geat. Historians know very little about the people that lived there. They may have been a tribe called the Gotar who lived in Jutland, which is now called Denmark. They were the enemies of the Swedes.

The Norsemen played an important role in the Middle Ages. They were bribed with lands by a French king who wanted to make peace with them. They settled in northern France, which came to be known as Normandy. These Norsemen came to be known as the Normans. They invaded England and conquered the Saxons. Many medieval stories grew up around these deeds.

The Vikings were Norsemen with a strong sense of adventure. They were expert seamen who discovered the Americas long before Columbus. They raided throughout Europe. Sometimes they killed and burned. Sometimes they made peace by marrying into a culture. Besides being raiders, the Vikings were traders. "To go Viking" means to sail off to war or adventure.

The Vikings had no written language. Like many ancient cultures, they never recorded their stories in written form. Storytellers were vital to the exchange of news, ideas, and customs. Their folklore has been passed down to us through the oral tradition. It was written by scholars many years after the Viking culture ceased to exist.

Metaphor and *alliteration* are often used in the Norse oral tradition. Metaphor is used by comparing one thing to another such as "Her hair was the sun." Alliteration is using similar sounds to create a literary effect, such as, "Screaming seagulls scraped the sky."

The Norse people also believed in hospitality to strangers and the generosity of kings and queens. A good king is often referred to as a "Gift-giver" or "Ring-giver."

Many early stories were originally written in poetic prose form—more like a poem than a story. One example is Beowulf, which takes place in Denmark. It was written in Britain around 750 A.D. in an old language called Anglo-Saxon. The Angles and the Saxons were tribes from Scandinavia and Germany.

The story of Beowulf is what we would call an *epic*: a long adventure with many parts. The stories in this book, "The Slaying of Grendel" and "Mother's Revenge," are only small parts of the epic poem *Beowulf*.

The epic begins with lengthy descriptions of the people and places in the story and ends after Beowulf slays Grendel's mother.

Charlemagne and the Crusades

A TALE FROM FRANCE

Roland the Mighty

oland was King Charlemagne's* favorite nephew. Being a favored relative of the king of France was not easy. Roland had enemies who were jealous of his position. He did not know that his greatest enemy was his own stepfather, Ganelon.*

Roland was a leader in the king's army. They were on crusade in Spain. He had helped the king win many battles against the Muslim armies. There was only one city left to defeat—the city of Sargossa.*

The ruler of this city was a wise man named Marsilla.* He decided against further bloodshed. He sent messengers to Charlemagne offering treasure if they could come to a peaceful solution.

Ganelon taunted Roland by saying, "Why do you not send your nephew, your Majesty? He will deliver your answer to the infidels." He laughed at his own cleverness. Ganelon hoped the infidels would kill Roland, and Ganelon would be rid of him for good. But King Charlemagne was more clever.

"I think a more seasoned man should go," replied the king. "You will go, Ganelon."

Ganelon was furious. He was determined to get revenge.

Marsilla welcomed the king's messenger and treated him with great respect. Ganelon plotted against the king and Roland.

"Your Majesty," Ganelon said to Marsilla. "I happen to know it would be quite easy for you to attack the Frankish king. You will succeed if you do as I say." While Marsilla desired peace, the suggestion of victory appealed to

* Charlemagne is pronounced *SHAR-luh-MANE*.
  Ganelon is pronounced *GAN-uh-lawn*.
  Sargossa is pronounced *sar-GOH-suh*.
  Marsilla is pronounced *mar-SIL-uh*.

him. He listened with interest. Ganelon's voice hissed like a snake as he delivered his plan.

Ganelon returned to Charlemagne with Marsilla's treasure. Ganelon told Charlemagne he could return to France, and Marsilla would pay him regular *tribute*.

Charlemagne led the main body homeward. Roland followed with the army's *rearguard*. As soon as Charlemagne was out of sight, the Muslims attacked. They isolated the rearguard from the rest of the Frankish army. The *Franks* were outnumbered but fought bravely. Again and again the Muslims attacked until Roland's men fell. The few left were trapped. They would fight or die, and Roland knew it.

Oliver, Roland's dearest friend and a brave knight, pleaded with him to blow his horn and summon Charlemagne. The king was their only hope. Almost all the Frankish knights had fallen.

"I will not!" shouted Roland, over the sound of clashing swords and screaming men.

"For the sake of our lives, Roland. Blow your horn!"

Roland ignored his friend. He chose to fight rather than to lose honor or endanger his uncle, the king.

Never has a battle been so fierce. Never have men fought so bravely. But in the end, they died. Roland, gravely wounded, leaned upon his sword. He raised the horn to his lips and gave a mighty blow. Miles away, Charlemagne held up his hand. His men listened, but they thought it was only the wind playing tricks with their ears. They marched on.

Again, Roland blew the horn. He blew so hard his temples burst. Blood ran down his cheeks and from his mouth. This time, the king knew it was his nephew's horn.

"He is in trouble!" shouted the king. He turned his horse around, and his army followed him at great speed.

A Muslim soldier rushed at Roland with his spear. Roland was slain before the last note sounded. The brave warrior fell beside his friend, Oliver.

Charlemagne crushed the remainder of the Muslim army, but he could not save Roland or the other knights of his realm. They were dead, brave and true to the end. They were buried with great honor.

May the mighty deeds of Roland live on as long as this tale is told. It is finished.

Tips for Telling

Point-of-view is very important in this story. During the crusades, the Muslims thought the Christian crusaders were a mannerless, dirty, violent people. The Christians thought the same thing of the Muslims. Both thought their own religion was the "true" one. This is a good example of how point-of-view can change a story.

The story of Roland is written from the Christian crusaders' point-of-view. It makes Roland out to be a hero and the Muslim king, Marsilla, to be the villain. You may want to consider other characters' points of view, such as Ganelon's. If you want to tell a story with a Muslim point-of-view, you will have to create a new story from this one, or tell the story of Saladin, a great Muslim leader.

Story History

The medieval church had wealth and power. Little was said or done without its knowledge. People in the Middle Ages were afraid of death, and the Church offered immortality through religion. If a man did the right things, was faithful to the church, and fought for God, he would be saved.

The crusades of the Middle Ages were religious campaigns or wars. Men and boys, and occasionally females, came from many countries offering their services as soldiers to fight against those they called *infidels*. In short, anyone who wasn't a Christian was considered an enemy of the Church. These were the crusades. And the crusaders' main enemies were the followers of Islam—the Moors, Turks, and Saracens.

There were many crusades, including a children's crusade. When the Muslims took control of the Holy City of Jerusalem, the Christians formed armies to fight against them. Ownership of the Holy Lands is still in dispute today. It is a center of religion for Jews, Christians, and Muslims.

It is important to know that the Muslims made many valuable contributions to the world. The lands occupied by them benefitted from high standards of architecture. They left behind many of the world's most beautiful structures. Quite often they would remodel Christian churches, and the Christians have done the same. This creates an astounding mixture of styles. The Muslims built cities with paved roads and other marvels unknown in European towns where roads were still made of mud.

The Muslims are also largely responsible for our knowledge of mathematics, medicine, astronomy, and other scientific developments. When the Christians and Muslims were on peaceful terms, the exchange of ideas was amazing. The Christians brought many wonderful bits of knowledge back to Europe, including the African/Arab game of Mancala.* This was a game they saw the Arabs playing. It became very popular in Europe at that time.

The Muslim leaders pushed and pushed into medieval Europe. They managed to build cities in Spain. This is where Roland's story takes place.

Hospitality was important to the Muslim people, and a law of war said a king's messenger was sacred. He was the voice of the king himself. This is why Ganelon was treated with respect when he took Charlemagne's message to Marsilla.

The king of France was Charles, or as he was known to the French people, Charlemagne. He was a strong and powerful king with many followers. And he was a successful soldier. His armies fought long and hard and finally overtook all but one city in northern Spain. That city was Sargossa.

The story of Roland was originally an epic poem, similar to that of Beowulf. One difference between the story of Beowulf and the story of Roland is that *Beowulf* is completely fiction. Roland is based on historical fact.

* Mancala is pronounced *man-CAW-luh*.

Saladin

A TALE FROM THE MUSLIMS

A Man of Honor

Two crusader prisoners were brought before the sultan, Saladin,* following the Battle of Hattin. One was Guy de Lusignan,* ruler of the kingdom of Jerusalem. The other was a dangerous man named Reginald de Chatillon.* Both men were noblemen deserving of Saladin's hospitality, but Chatillon was not a man of honor in the sultan's eyes.

Chatillon held a castle at the edge of the desert. From there he attacked, insulted, and abused innocent Muslim pilgrims and caravans. Chatillon had broken a truce. Now he was at Saladin's mercy.

The great leader looked at his prisoners. "You are thirsty from your journey to my tent," said Saladin.

He ordered a servant to pour a cup of cool water in front of his hostages. He handed the cup to Guy de Lusignan. Guy eagerly accepted the drink and thanked his host. Guy then handed the cup to his friend Reginald. But before Reginald's hands could grasp the cup, Saladin stepped between them.

He bowed in respect to Guy. "Your royal person is sacred, but this man…" he said turning to Chatillon. "He is a ruffian and a man without honor. He is not worthy of my cup."

Upon saying this, Saladin slew Reginald.

Aside: Some may think Saladin was a cruel man. You must decide for yourself if he was a good judge.

---

* Saladin is pronounced *SAL-uh-din*.
  Guy de Lusignan is pronounced *GEE duh loo-zeen-YON*.
  Chatillon is pronounced *shot-ee-YON*.

Tips for Telling

This story is not recommended for very young children. I would tell this one to grade five and up.

If you do not tell the story of Roland, you may want to explain a little about the crusades and who fought in them—Muslims and Christians. You may also want to tell a little about Saladin before or after your story.

You may want to find ways to describe the characters so you don't have to pronounce their names each time. They are difficult names. *Example*: You might call Guy de Lusignan "Sir Guy" or "the King of Jerusalem." You can call Reginald "the traitor."

Story History

This story takes place just before the Third Crusade. It is based on facts following the Battle of Hattin. Later, Saladin took Jerusalem, and King Richard Lion-Heart led the Third Crusade against him.

Historians still consider Saladin, or Salah ad-Din, one the best military men of all time. He is highly respected as a man of honor and valor. Even King Richard admired him. He appears to have been just and generous. History says that he was not a greedy man. He was a warrior for his religion, not for profit. He never even built a palace for himself. He died a man without possessions.

Alexander the Great

A TALE FROM GREECE

The Gordian Knot

*G*ordius, the first king of Phrygia,* left a puzzle for future kings and warriors to solve. It was a knot that tied his *oxcart* to a *yoke*. The knot had no visible ends. It was known as the Gordian Knot. It made the city of Phrygia famous.

During ancient times, many men asked for signs from magicians and the *Oracle at Delphi.** The Oracle could see into the future. The Oracle said, "Whoever removes the Gordian Knot will rule the world."

One day Alexander visited Phrygia. He was only in his twenties but was already a mighty ruler and military leader. He had conquered all of Greece, but that was not enough. He was on his way to conquer other lands. Alexander would have passed by the small city of Phrygia, but it was considered unlucky to pass without at least trying to untie the knot. Thousands of men had tried. All had failed.

Alexander went to the temple of Jupiter where the oxcart was kept. He circled it, studied it with a keen eye, then circled it again.

Without even taking his eyes from the knot he asked one of his generals, "Is this the great Gordian Knot?"

His general replied, "It is."

Before the words left his general's lips, Alexander drew his sword. With one swift slash, the knot fell open.

Alexander did what others could not do. He was a problem solver. Alexander went on to conquer the whole *known world*.

---

* Phrygia is pronounced *FRIJ-ee-uh*.
  Delphi is pronounced *DELF-eye*.

Tips for Telling

Look for places in the story to speak more excitingly. And at other places, speak slowly to build suspense, especially as Alexander studies the knot. Speed up your words when you describe how he cut it with his sword and went on to conquer the known world.

Story History

Alexander was from Macedonia.* This story takes place during his conquests of Persia. Persia no longer exists. It is now Turkey, Iraq, Iran, Lebanon, and Syria, among other small countries in that area. This story is told from the winner's point of view—the Greeks. Most of the people living in Persia at that time feared Alexander and called him a demon. He stole their great treasures and destroyed many beautiful buildings and artworks. Many people living in the area today still dislike him, including storytellers in Iran who still tell his tale!

Alexander came from a time of politics and war. His father was a king. His mother was also politically-minded. She wanted her son to be king after his father. Some historians even think she and Alexander planned his father's murder.

Alexander had a good teacher. His father sent him to study with Aristotle, one of history's greatest thinkers. Like many conquerors, Alexander was ambitious and cruel as well as wise. Alexander became sick when he was only thirty-two years old and died. His empire fell apart after his death.

This story took place before the Middle Ages, but storytellers may have told this tale during the medieval period. Any of the Greek, Roman, or Egyptian myths would also be good stories to tell as a medieval storyteller, since they happened prior to the Middle Ages.

* Macedonia is pronounced MASS-uh-DOH-nee-uh.

Eleanor of Aquitaine

A TALE FROM ENGLAND

The Queen Checks the King

The Queen of England waited in her castle prison. Yes, it was a castle with every comfort, but it was still a prison. Her husband, Henry, King of England, put her there because he was afraid of her power. How many years had it been? Sixteen? It seemed like a long time since she was free. How she missed those years.

When news of Henry's death came, Eleanor was shocked. First she wept. Then she laughed. Her son Richard would be king and set his mother free. "He always was a thoughtful boy," Eleanor said to herself. Now her maids packed the queen's clothes. They were going home.

"I wonder," she said to her maids, "if they will remember the old days–the *troubadours*,* I mean?" The queen laughed. "Or will they sing of a queen whose husband used her for politics and show?"

Her personal handmaid replied, "They will remember, your Majesty. You will always be their queen." She wrapped a cloak about the queen's shoulders.

When the door opened, Eleanor of Aquitaine* stepped into a strange England, but it was still her England. She was still a woman of power. And, although she was sixty-seven years old, she was still quite lovely. No one could say Henry took anything from her but his love and her freedom. At least she had her freedom again.

Eleanor was a proud woman and a respected queen. She watched as her son was crowned Richard Lion-Heart, King of England. It was Eleanor who sat as *regent** until her son was old enough to take the throne. It was

---

* Troubadours is pronounced *TRUE-buh-doors*.
  Aquitaine is pronounced *AW-quih-tayne*.
  Regent is pronounced *REE-junt*.

Eleanor who helped raise money for his release from Austria following the crusades. And it was Eleanor who was buried beside two kings—her son, Richard, and her husband, Henry.

Yet few people know her greatest secret: how she cheered quietly for the prisoners when Richard released them from *gaol** upon his father's death. She loved that one joke on her husband. She wondered, what would he have said about that? And about her own release?

Eleanor was queen of two countries and mother to two kings. Nothing ever stopped her—not even a palace prison or a frightened king. She was the queen who checked the king. In the end, she won the game.

Tips for Telling

This is a more historical story than many others in this book. One responsibility of the medieval storyteller was to tell histories and honor the noble men and women. When you tell this story, you might think of yourself as a troubadour in Eleanor's court. The story might sound as if you are looking back and remembering someone you admired. You might also read about Henry and Eleanor and tell the story from the king's viewpoint. He admired his wife but did not trust her political power. His story would be a very different story.

Story History

During the Middle Ages, women had little, if any power. Women and children were considered the property of men. Few women married for love. Most marriages were arranged for political and economic reasons. Even Eleanor of Aquitaine had an arranged marriage. But Eleanor was still an exceptional woman. She was outspoken when many women were silent.

When her parents died, Eleanor was just fifteen years old and became Duchess of Aquitaine, the largest province in all France. She was soon married to Louis, King of France, and traveled with him on crusade to the holy lands. Her husband divorced her because she had no male children. This happened quite a lot in medieval Europe. She was forced to leave her daughters with Louis.

* Gaol is pronounced *JAIL*.

Even without her husband, Eleanor still ruled the largest part of France. She returned home to Aquitaine and opened a court at Poitiers.* Medieval courts were not like our modern legal court. Holding court was more like a business meeting. Sometimes, the king or queen made laws and decisions about punishments in court. Lesser lords paid their tributes here as well. There were no juries. The king's or queen's word was final. Court was also a place where artisans and politicians gathered to gain favor with the royalty. The best of all troubadours came to Eleanor's court to sing of the queen's beauty and grace. Eleanor was a *patron* of the arts.

A short time later she married Henry II, King of England. The royal couple had several children. Among them were William, who was their first. William should have been king when his father died, but he died in infancy. There were two daughters, Matilda and Joanna. There were four other boys: Richard, Geoffrey, John, and Henry. Of course, you recognize two of their boys—Richard Lion-Heart and John, who later became known as John Lackland, because he had no lands. (He lacked them.) Medieval names came from places like Eleanor of Aquitaine, or deeds like Richard Lion-Heart, or from things like physical features such as Little John.

Eleanor and Henry argued over which of their sons should be king after the two oldest died. Eleanor favored Richard. Henry preferred John. At one time, her sons persuaded her to help them raise a rebellion against their father. Eleanor's position of power and wealth made her a dangerous woman. She had influence. So, Henry put her in prison. After his death, Eleanor was released by her son, Richard, and at age sixty-seven became his helper in running the kingdom. She died at age eighty-two.

---

* Poitiers is pronounced *pwah-tee-AY*.

Boudicca

A TALE FROM THE CELTS

Queen of the Iceni

Boudicca's* husband, the king, was dead. She had two daughters. She was now ruler of her people, the Iceni.*

One day, after her husband was killed in battle, Roman soldiers came. They pulled her from her house. They whipped the queen and treated her daughters poorly. The wealth and lands of her people were destroyed. The people themselves were enslaved or killed.

"This," they said, "is to remind you that we are the rulers in your land." Then they laughed. They left the queen to pick up the broken pieces of her life.

They did not know how strong and powerful Boudicca was. She did not give up. Instead, she raised an army within the Iceni. Soon, other tribes of Celts joined them. Within days, Boudicca's armies attacked and looted some of the Romans' largest cities, including the colony of London. They took no prisoners. They destroyed and burned the Roman towns.

After many battles, the Roman leaders became furious. They decided to trap Boudicca. Her army was larger than theirs, but they were more skilled. The Romans waited until Boudicca's forces were in a narrow valley between the Roman army and the Celts' own supply wagons. The Roman forces attacked and killed men, women, and children. The queen escaped in her chariot with her daughters.

When the Romans caught up with the queen, she and her daughters were already dead. Boudicca cheated the Romans of the satisfaction of her capture. She became an inspiration for the Celts for all time. Boudicca was a brave and proud queen.

---

* Boudicca is pronounced *boo-DEE-kuh*.
  Iceni is pronounced *eye-SEE-nee*.

Tips for Telling

This story is written from a Celtic viewpoint. The Romans were invaders who took their lands, their identity, and their culture. This story may be told from the Roman point-of-view. To the Romans, the Celts were a rough people who were not able to band together for any reason other than destruction. You may choose to tell the story from a neutral point-of-view. To do this, you should be careful not to make either side look good or bad. History tells us that the Celts killed men, women, and children, but so did the Romans' troops. Each side had its way of life and its beliefs. Both sides could be brutal.

You may also want to put in more battle details.

Story History

The story of Boudicca happens before the Middle Ages, around the year 61 AD. The country we now know as Great Britain (Ireland, Scotland, Wales, and England) was once inhabited by the Keltoi or Celts (pronounced with a "K" sound, not an "S." The "S"eltics are a basketball team. The "K"elts are the people of Ireland, Scotland, and Wales). These people had a rich ancient history out of which grew many stories, such as the tales of King Arthur. The Celts actually lived all throughout what is now called Europe, in France, Germany, Spain, Italy, and elsewhere. But the isles of Great Britain are where they eventually settled. Although Ireland was difficult to invade due to its rough seas and cliffs, England was invaded by the Romans, who crossed the channel as early as 55 BC. The Celts did not give up their identity easily, though, and fought the Romans, then later the Saxons.

Yet the Romans made many contributions to Britain's history. They built cities and paved roads. These can still be seen. London is one of the Roman cities.

The Romans were shrewd invaders. Instead of killing everyone, they tried to turn the inhabitants into Roman citizens. Some of the Celts resisted.

When Boudicca's husband died, his lands were divided between his wife and the Romans. This was the Roman law, and the Celts agreed to it to keep the peace. However, the Romans were not satisfied, and this is what started the war with Boudicca, the Iceni queen, who was not willing to let the Romans take it all.

Something else to keep in mind: the Celtic women fought in battle right beside the men. It was quite often the women who trained the men for battle. Women also owned property and had a voice in politics. The Celts were known as excellent horsemen and skilled charioteers. They were fierce in battle and not easy to defeat. While the Romans thought of them as heathens, they admired the Celts skill and prowess.

Storytelling Pointers

The Medieval Storyteller

Storytellers of the Middle Ages were news reporters. They were educators and entertainers. The spoken word was powerful. A story about a king's generosity—or his stinginess—could spread like wildfire if told by a good storyteller. Storytellers were treated with respect and given the best a *nobleman* could offer. They were paid with food, rest, and gold. A noble family might even keep a *bard* in its household to sing or tell the praises of that noble and his history. These bards lived and traveled with that noble. Other storytellers might wander freely from place to place spreading tales. Their stories came from many sources, even other cultures they visited.

Because storytelling was a spoken art form, tales changed from place to place and teller to teller. That is one reason so many stories seem alike but may also be quite different from each other. Many of them were not written down until many years later. The storyteller relied on his or her memory for the facts.

Another reason many stories sound alike is that most people have similar experiences in life. There will be some things you will have to explain to the audience and some things we all have in common. Part of your job as a storyteller is to look for those things. When you find common experiences among people, you will find your audience more interested in the stories.

You may have to change or explain those things in the story that are different in your culture. Sometimes, storytellers changed names, places, and who the heroes or villains were in a story. This has to do with point-of-view. All of this is part of your job as a storyteller.

How to be a Medieval Storyteller

Deciding who is telling the story is called point-of-view. This can be fun. Storytellers are narrators and characters when they tell a story. If you choose to be a medieval storyteller, you will also be someone from history. You will be a storyteller pretending to be a medieval person. You will have medieval opinions. A woman would think in a different way than a man because their roles were different. And their ideas were different from ours today. This would also be true of people from different religions, countries, and social classes.

Example: If you are telling the story of Joan of Arc and you are English, you would think she was dangerous. If you are French, she would be a hero. If you are a man, you would think she should not have so much power. If you are a woman, you might feel proud of her. A person of nobility might laugh at her. A peasant might be envious or proud.

To help with viewpoint, ask yourself, "How would I feel about this story if I lived in the Middle Ages?" The story will be more interesting if you think like a medieval person. To determine who is telling the story, you might first develop a *persona* for yourself. Who are you? Man? Woman? Child? Rich? Poor? Monk? Nun? Where do you live? How do you think?

Watch out for modern words like "cool." Try words such as "splendid," "marvelous," or "wondrous." Your character will be more believable. Also try not to use contractions, such as "you're" or "can't." Use "you are" and "cannot." Language in the Middle Ages did not have contractions. Most noble men and women spoke formally. You may want to change the word "will" to "shall."

Although peasants used slang, their words were different from ours, so try to avoid using modern slang. Peasants also had poor grammar.

You may consider dressing as a medieval storyteller. In the Middle Ages, it was improper to show much of the human body. The human body was considered earthly, and the church expected people to think more about heaven. Ladies did not show their ankles or their elbows. And a proper lady always kept her head covered. Besides, it was practical to cover your head if you were in the working class. That kept the dirt out of your hair. Remember most people didn't bathe very often in the Middle Ages either.

Lords and ladies of nobility showed off their wealth by the fine clothes they wore. Ladies wore their dresses long, so that the trains dragged on the floor. It was a sign of wealth, as were long flowing sleeves. Lords sometimes wore tights with jerkins or tunics, and they often wore "dresses" much like the ladies' garb.

Peasants had a different type of outlook on their clothes. They had to make their own from handspun and handwoven goods, so they were lucky to own one piece of clothing. It was usually short—no more than ankle-length, if not shorter. This way they could move about easily without tripping over their clothes. If a piece of clothing were ruined, it was sewn or patched. Even a fine lady's clothes were seldom thrown away, but instead were made over for someone or something else.

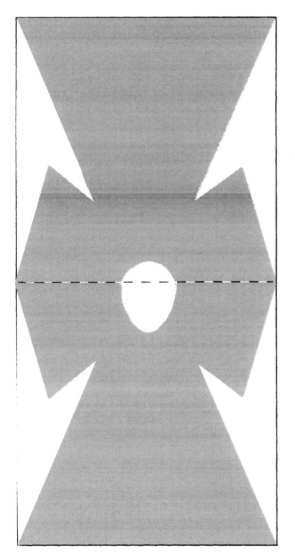

THE BASIC "T"

The "T" tunic is cut from a single piece of fabric. The seam runs under each arm and down the sides. There is no seam at the shoulders.

The yardage will vary depending on the length of the tunic, the width of the fabric, and the sleeve length.

Make a pattern for the neck hole (see variations below) and modify as needed. It works best when the neck hole is off-center with more opening to the front.

You will need to round the hemlines slightly unless you want peaks at the sides.

Layering tunics was common— especially for the ruling classes—so you may want to make two or more tunics of varying lengths for layering. And leftover fabric is great for pouches, belts, and headpieces.

Use rustic open-weave fabrics for work and peasant garb and tightly woven fancy fabric for noble garb.

Your Job as a Storyteller

I. Know your audience

One of your jobs is to find things the audience has in common with the characters in the stories. This will help them become more interested in your story and understand it better. This is very important if you are telling stories to people older or younger than yourself. If your audience is younger or knows less about your topic, you will have to explain some things. You can do this before or during your story, as an *aside*. You can also include the information as part of the story. It is different if your audience is older. You can use what you know about them to tell the story.

Example: You are telling the story of William Tell who shoots an arrow off the top of his own son's head. You could use an aside to the adults by asking a question such as, "How many of you would do that?" You may get some very funny answers.

For younger children, you might say, "Do you think that boy was brave? He trusted his father."

II. Get the audience's attention and keep it

Look at the audience. Make each person feel you are talking to him or her. If you look at floors, walls, or ceilings, you may lose the audience's attention. Storytelling is different from acting. In acting, you can't talk to the audience because you are a character in the play. When you tell stories, you can talk to the audience.

Here are some tips for better storytelling.

a. Stand in front of the audience.

b. Look at each person. Take your time. Make sure they know you are there before you begin your story. You are in charge. Show this by standing straight with your shoulders back and balancing evenly on both feet. You may want to tip your chin up a little and lean slightly forward. Take a deep breath, and begin when you are ready.

c. Control your space. You can change the seats or the way the room is set up. You can change where you have to stand or sit. Do this before you start.

d. Make sure everyone can see you. Be careful not to make the audience look into the sun or any bright light. It will hurt their eyes. You don't want people walking into the room behind you or looking out the window. Plan where to stand or sit.

e. Stand up so everyone can see you, or sit on a tall stool. Sit at eye level for small children who are sitting on the floor. It will hurt their necks if you stand up. You want them to be comfortable.

f. Speak up. Talk to the back of the room. It is common to speed up when you are nervous, so remind yourself to slow down. Pronounce your words clearly.

g. Try to remain still so the audience won't become distracted from the story. Sometimes gestures help an audience "see" the story better, but they're not necessary. If you are sitting, lean toward the audience and sit on the edge of your chair. This will help your voice carry and keep the audience's attention.

III. Have fun with the audience

Watch what they are doing. Do they seem really interested in something? Are they laughing? Give them time to laugh. Change the tone and volume of your voice to keep their attention focused on your words. Interact with them. Take good care of your audience and enjoy them.

IV. Be true to the story

The story is the most important part of a storyteller's performance. Watch out for things that take away from the story, such as unnecessary movements. Your most important job is to pass the story along to others. They need to be able to hear it and understand it.

Glossary

Alliteration: using repeated sounds for effect:
   The poor peasants pondered their predicament

Aside: when the teller stops the story and explains something directly to the audience

Avalon: a mythological island surrounded by mist; thought to be the home of the Sidhe and magic

Balladeers: people who make story-songs called ballads

Bards: a word used by the Celts for storytellers, singers, and poets

Camelot: the mythological city Arthur built in honor of his wife, Guenevere

Celtic: someone born of Irish, Welsh, or Scottish blood

Courtiers: people of nobility living with the royal family; people living at the nobleman's court

Dauphin: what the French people called their prince

Druid: an ancient Celtic priest

Epic: a long story, often in poetic form, that usually gives the history of the characters before and after the main events of the story

Field: background color and/or design of a banner or shield

Franks: an early Germanic tribe that settled in France

Freeborn peasant: a man or woman born into a freeman's household who worked the land for the noblemen or owned small businesses; they had more freedom than the serfs but still had to follow the noble's laws

Gaol: jail

Gordius: a peasant who became king of Phrygia

Guild: a union consisting of artisans such as the weaver's guild; apprentices and journeymen operated under supervision of a master artisan

Heresy: disobeying the law of the Church

Infidels: a term used by the Christians and the Muslims when speaking about each other; it refers to anyone not of the "true" faith

Known world: the extent of the world as it was known during the Middle Ages and Renaissance

Metaphor: using one word or phase to describe something, such as saying, "The water was a sea of diamonds" instead of "It sparkled"

Moor: open, rolling, marshy wasteland

Mutton: lamb

Nobleman: anyone given a title by the king; titles usually passed through the family

Oracle at Delphi: the oracle was the prophetess of the earth goddess Gaea, said to have the power to see the future; she was located in Greece at Delphi

Oxcart: a cart pulled by oxen instead of horses

Patron: someone who supported artists with money and work

Peasant: a poor man or woman who could be a serf or free

Persona: a person or character one pretends to be

Quarterstaff: a long thick pole used for fighting

Rearguard: a section of the army that followed the main body of the army to protect it from attack from behind

Regent: a person of nobility assigned to run the kingdom during the absence of the king; similar to a vice president

Serf: a worker for the noble who cared for the land; serfs had no freedoms and were almost like slaves—they even needed permission to travel and marry

Tartars: people of Turkish origin who invaded Asia and Europe under Mongol leadership during the thirteenth century

Tribute: a sum of money or other payment given to the noble of the land; taxes

Troubadours: singing poets who often lived at court to sing the praises of the nobles

Yoke: a wooden harness strapped between two cows, oxen, or horses when pulling a cart

Source Notes

WILLIAM TELL

This is one of the first medieval legends I heard as a child. I have used my memory of the story and the following source.

Baldwin, James. *Arrow Book of Famous Stories*. New York: Scholastic Magazines, 1963.

ROBERT BRUCE AND THE SPIDER

Baldwin, James. *Arrow Book of Famous Stories*. New York: Scholastic Magazines, 1963.

———. *Fifty Favorite Stories Retold*. New York: American Book Company, 1924.

French, Marion N. *Myths and Legends of the Ages*. New York: Hart Book Company, 1951.

ROBIN HOOD

Bulfinch, Thomas. *The Age of Chivalry and Legends of Charlemagne*. New York: Penguin, 1995.

Cox, John Harrington. *The Young Folk's Shelf of Books*. New York: Collier, n.d.

Osbourne, Mary Pope and Troy Howell. *Favorite Medieval Tales*. New York: Scholastic Press, 1998.

Sterling, Sara Hawks. *Robin Hood and His Merry Men*. Philadelphia: Macrae Smith Company, 1921.

JOAN OF ARC

I grew up reading about Joan and watching movies about her. I have been telling her story since the early 1990s. My version is a little different from the one I present here. When I tell her story, I tell it from the point of view of a woman whose husband fought in Joan's army.

KING ARTHUR

Ashe, Geoffrey. *The Discovery of King Arthur*. New York: Anchor Press/Doubleday, 1985.

Bulfinch, Thomas. *The Age of Chivalry and Legends of Charlemagne*. New York: Penguin, 1995.

Cox, John Harrington. *The Young Folk's Shelf of Books*. New York: Collier, n.d.

Jennings, Philip S. *Medieval Legends*. New York: St. Martin's Press, 1983.

Osbourne, Mary Pope and Troy Howell. *Favorite Medieval Tales*. New York: Scholastic Press, 1998.

LECH AND THE NEST

Anstruther, F.C. *Old Polish Legends*. New York: Hippocrene Books, 1991.

Uminski, Sigmund H. *Tales of Early Poland*. Detroit: Endurance Press, 1968.

Boronczyk, Timothy. "Poland—Historical Flags: The Origins of the White Eagle of Poland." 1999 [cited 8 March 2000]. Available from www.fotw.net/flags/pl-hist.html#eagle.

"Inside Poland: The Basics: Topics: National Symbols: National Emblem." In Global Technology Integration. 1998-1999 [cited 16 Aug 1999]. Available from www.inside-poland.pl.

BEOWULF

Cox, John Harrington. *The Young Folk's Shelf of Books*. New York: Collier, n.d.

Goodrich, Norma Lorre. *Medieval Myths*. New York: Penguin, 1961.

Osbourne, Mary Pope and Troy Howell. *Favorite Medieval Tales*. New York: Scholastic Press, 1998.

Breeden, Dr. David. "Beowulf Legend: The Adventures of Beowulf." 1999 [cited 16 Aug 1999]. Available from www.lone-star.net/literature/beowulf/beowulf.html.

"Beowulf." In Encarta Encyclopedia from MSN Microsoft. 1997-1999 [cited 16 Aug 1999]. Available from encarta.msn.com.

CHARLEMAGNE

Goodrich, Norma Lorre. *Medieval Myths*. New York: Penguin, 1961.

Osbourne, Mary Pope and Troy Howell. *Favorite Medieval Tales*. New York: Scholastic Press, 1998.

Sayers, Dorothy L., trans. *The Song of Roland*. New York: Penguin Classics, 1957.

Williams, Jay. *The Horn of Roland*. New York: Thomas Y. Crowell Company, 1968.

Yuan, Derek. "The Song of Roland: Analysis of the French Masterpiece." 1998 [cited 16–18 Aug 1999]. www.enloe.wake.k12.nc.us/enloe/CandC/france/franceindex.html.

SALADIN

Maalouf, Amin. *The Crusades Through Arab Eyes*. New York: Schocken Books, 1983.

"Egypt History: Ayyubid Rule (1171-1250)." In ArabNet Reproduction. 1996 [cited 18 Aug 1999]. Available from www.arab.net/egypt/history/et_ayyubid.html.

"Cairo History Guide: The Age of Saladin (1168-1250)." 1997 [cited 18 Aug 1999]. Available from ce.eng.usf.edu/pharos/cairo/history/saladin.html.

Halsall, Paul. "Medieval Sourcebook: The Capture of Jerusalem by Saladin 1187." 1997 [cited 18 Aug 1999]. Available from www.fordham.edu/halsall/source/1187saladin.html.

"Infoplease.com: Saladin." In Kid's Almanac. 1993 [cited 18 Aug 1999]. Available from http://kids.infoplease.com/ipka/A0001215.html.

Kjeilen, Tore. "Encyclopedia of the Orient: Saladin." Cited 18 Aug 1999. Available from i-Cias.com/e.o/.

"The Novels of Sir Walter Scott—The Talisman." Notes. In Waverly Novels—The Centenary Edition, Vol. 3. Cited 18 Aug 1999. Available from www2.arts.gla.ac.uk/www/english/comet/starn/prose/wscott/talisman/notes.htm.

ALEXANDER THE GREAT AND THE GORIDAN KNOT

"Athens: Alexander the Great, King of Macedonia." In Geocities. 1998 [cited 17 Aug 1999]. Available from www.geocities.com/Athens/Aegean/7545/Alexander.html.

"Gordian Knot." In Encarta Encyclopedia from MSN Microsoft. Cited 16 Aug 1999. Available from encarta.msn.com.

ELEANOR OF AQUITAINE

Because I love stories of Robin Hood, I have also read about King Richard the Lionheart who plays a role in Robin's stories. Richard's mother, Eleanor, played a role in Richard's story. I have used the following source plus information from years of medieval study to create her story.

Walker, Curtis Howe. *Eleanor of Aquitaine*. New York: Lancer Books, 1950.

BOUDICCA

"Description by Tacitus of the Rebellion of Boudicca (AD 60-61)." In Athena Review Vol. 1, No. 1. 1996 [cited 17 Aug 1999]. Available from www.athenapub.com/tacitus1.htm.

Jensen, Olivia. "Boadicea (Boudica)." 1998 [cited 17 Aug 1999]. Available from travesti.geophys.mcgill.ca/ ~ olivia/BOUDICA/.

Made in the USA
Middletown, DE
26 May 2018